ON NOVEMBER 13, 1780, IN THE SMALL TOWN OF BUDRUKHAN NEAR JIND, RAJ KAUR GAVE BIRTH TO A BOY WHO WAS DESTINED TO BE GREAT. HE WAS CALLED RANJIT SINGH.

THE RIVER WAS SWIFT AND ROUGH BUT RANJIT WAS ITS EQUAL.

ONCE WHEN RANJIT WAS STILL QUITE YOUNG—

WHAT IS WRONG WITH HIM, DOCTOR?

I AM AFRAID HE HAS SMALL POX.

AFTER MANY ANXIOUS DAYS—

WILL HE LIVE, DOCTOR?

YES, BUT HE WILL BE BLIND IN HIS LEFT EYE.

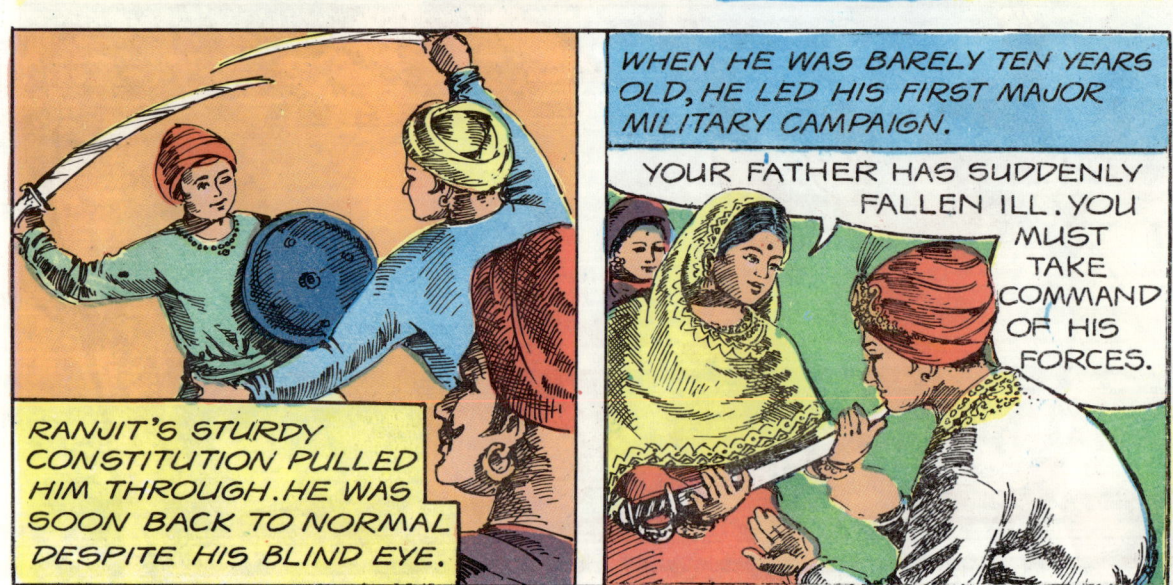

RANJIT'S STURDY CONSTITUTION PULLED HIM THROUGH. HE WAS SOON BACK TO NORMAL DESPITE HIS BLIND EYE.

WHEN HE WAS BARELY TEN YEARS OLD, HE LED HIS FIRST MAJOR MILITARY CAMPAIGN.

YOUR FATHER HAS SUDDENLY FALLEN ILL. YOU MUST TAKE COMMAND OF HIS FORCES.

A REBELLIOUS CHIEF HAD USURPED TERRITORY BELONGING TO RANJIT'S FATHER.

SIRE, MAHAN SINGH IS ILL AND HIS SON HAS BEEN SENT TO OVERTHROW US.

THAT TEN-YEAR-OLD BOY! HA! HA! HA!

BUT RANJIT WAS NO ORDINARY TEN-YEAR-OLD BOY.

BOMBARD THE MAIN GATE.

BUT—

WE ARE BEING ATTACKED FROM BEHIND, MASTER!

INSPIRED, RANJIT SINGH'S TROOPS RENEWED THE ASSAULT ON THE FORT.

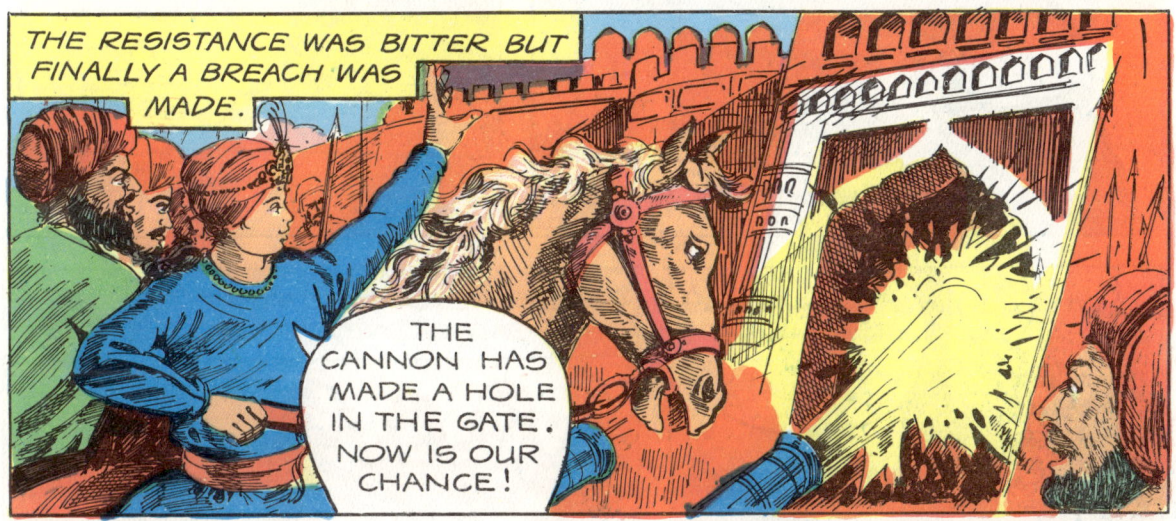

THE RESISTANCE WAS BITTER BUT FINALLY A BREACH WAS MADE.

THE CANNON HAS MADE A HOLE IN THE GATE. NOW IS OUR CHANCE!

FORWARD! MY MEN!

THE DEMORALISED ENEMY SOON SURRENDERED.

I NEVER THOUGHT I WOULD BE DEFEATED BY A TEN-YEAR-OLD BOY!

BUT THE VICTORY WAS TINGED WITH TRAGEDY.

MASTER, I HAVE SAD NEWS.

WHAT IS IT?

YOUR FATHER IS DEAD!

RANJIT RETURNED HOME TO A SAD SCENE.

THE FOLLOWING YEAR, RANJIT SINGH NARROWLY ESCAPED AN ATTEMPT ON HIS LIFE.

HIS WELL-TRAINED HORSE REARED UP AND SAVED HIM.

THIS LUCKY BREAK WAS ALL THAT RANJIT SINGH NEEDED.

WHEN HE WAS FIFTEEN, RANJIT SINGH MARRIED A DAUGHTER OF KANHAYAS, A POWERFUL SIKH FAMILY.

HE SOON CAME UNDER THE INFLUENCE OF HIS MOTHER-IN-LAW, SADA KAUR, A REMARKABLE WOMAN.

I HAVE GREAT HOPES FOR YOU, RANJIT!

SHE URGED RANJIT SINGH TO BECOME THE RULER OF A UNITED PUNJAB.

THE PUNJAB NEEDS ONE RULER.

I SHALL MAKE THE OTHER CHIEFTAINS SUBMIT TO ME.

BUT BEFORE RANJIT SINGH COULD PROCEED, A NEW THREAT ENGAGED HIS ATTENTION.

10

THOUGH HEAVILY OUTNUMBERED, RANJIT SINGH DECIDED TO FACE THE MIGHTY AFGHANS. THE OVER-CONFIDENT AFGHANS WERE BEATEN BY A DETERMINED OPPONENT.

THE WHOLE OF THE PUNJAB WAS ELATED BY RANJIT SINGH'S GREAT VICTORY.

AT LAST WE HAVE FOUND A GREAT LEADER!

BUT WILL THE OTHER CHIEFS SUBMIT TO HIM.

THERE IS A DELEGATION OF CITIZENS FROM LAHORE TO SEE YOU.

WE HAVE BEEN DEPUTED BY THE CITIZENS OF LAHORE TO ASK YOU TO TAKE OVER OUR CITY.

LAHORE WAS THE POLITICAL CAPITAL OF THE PUNJAB. CONTROL OF THAT CITY WAS ESSENTIAL IF RANJIT SINGH WERE TO BECOME MASTER OF THE PUNJAB.

BRING MORE WINE!

LAHORE WAS RULED BY THREE SARDARS. FORTUNATELY FOR RANJIT SINGH, THEY WERE A DISSOLUTE LOT AND THE PEOPLE WERE DISILLUSIONED BY THEM.

THE SARDARS SPEND OUR HARD-EARNED MONEY ON WINE AND WOMEN!

I BELIEVE A DELEGATION HAS ASKED RANJIT SINGH TO OUST THEM AND TAKE THEIR PLACE!

WITH THE BACKING OF THE PEOPLE OF LAHORE, RANJIT SINGH TOOK OVER THE CITY. HIS FIRST PUBLIC ACT WAS TO PAY HOMAGE AT THE BADSHAHI MOSQUE.

THOUGH RANJIT SINGH IS A SIKH, HE RESPECTS THE MUSLIMS.

YES, MANY MUSLIMS ARE NOW FIGHTING IN HIS ARMY.

RANJIT SINGH NEXT SUBDUED THE RAJA OF JAMMU.

ON BAISAKHI (APRIL 12), 1801, RANJIT SINGH WAS DECLARED MAHARAJA OF THE PUNJAB.

LONG LIVE THE MAHARAJA!

AFTER HIS CORONATION, RANJIT SINGH RODE ON AN ELEPHANT THROUGH THE STREETS OF LAHORE, SHOWERING COINS ON THE JUBILANT CROWD.

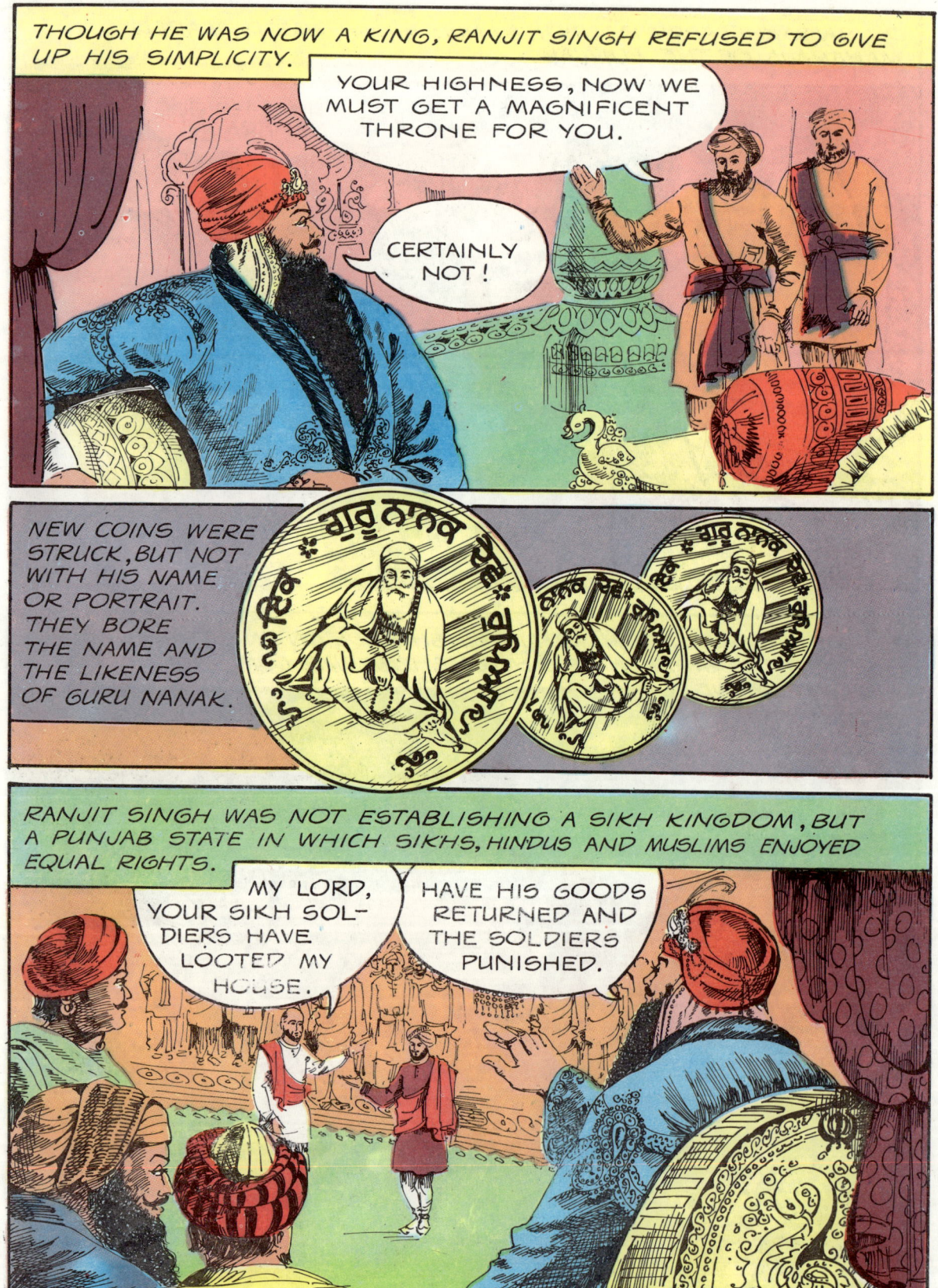

THOUGH HE WAS NOW A KING, RANJIT SINGH REFUSED TO GIVE UP HIS SIMPLICITY.

YOUR HIGHNESS, NOW WE MUST GET A MAGNIFICENT THRONE FOR YOU.

CERTAINLY NOT!

NEW COINS WERE STRUCK, BUT NOT WITH HIS NAME OR PORTRAIT. THEY BORE THE NAME AND THE LIKENESS OF GURU NANAK.

RANJIT SINGH WAS NOT ESTABLISHING A SIKH KINGDOM, BUT A PUNJAB STATE IN WHICH SIKHS, HINDUS AND MUSLIMS ENJOYED EQUAL RIGHTS.

MY LORD, YOUR SIKH SOLDIERS HAVE LOOTED MY HOUSE.

HAVE HIS GOODS RETURNED AND THE SOLDIERS PUNISHED.

HE TOOK PART IN THE RELIGIOUS FESTIVALS OF ALL THE COMMUNITIES. DURING DASSEHRA, HE PARTICIPATED IN THE SYMBOLIC BURNING OF RAVANA.

ON ID, HE VISITED HIS MUSLIM FRIENDS.

ON GURU NANAK'S BIRTHDAY, HE BATHED WITH HIS FAMILY AND MEMBERS OF THE SIKH COMMUNITY AT THE AMRITSAR GOLDEN TEMPLE.

RANJIT SINGH'S COURT REFLECTED HIS SECULAR NATURE.

RANJIT SINGH NEEDED TREATMENT FOR HIS EYE.

MY EYE HAS BEEN TROUBLING ME!

CALL AZIZUDDIN. HE IS SUPPOSED TO BE AN EXCELLENT DOCTOR.

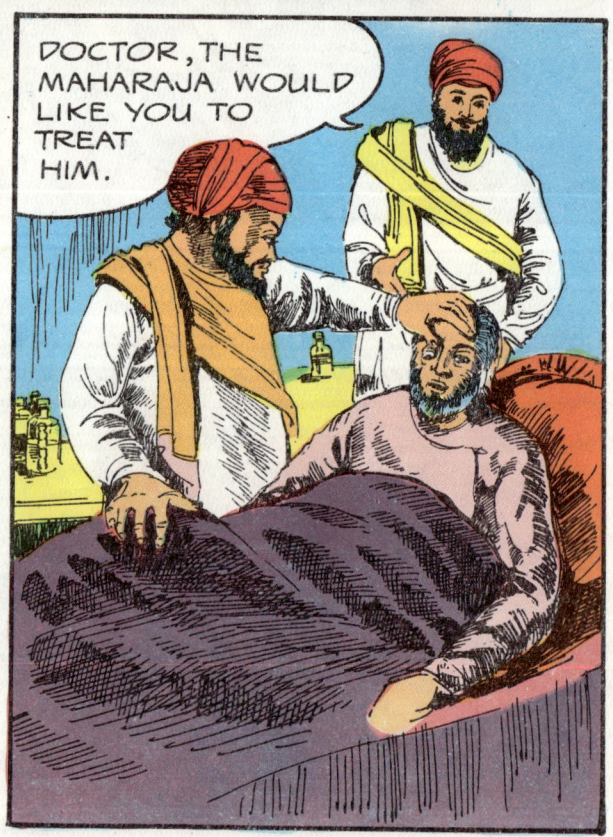

DOCTOR, THE MAHARAJA WOULD LIKE YOU TO TREAT HIM.

I SHALL GIVE YOU SOME DROPS WHICH SHOULD CURE THE TROUBLE.

RANJIT SINGH'S EYE IMPROVED AND SOON AZIZ BECAME A REGULAR VISITOR TO RANJIT SINGH'S COURT. ONE DAY—

YOU ARE AN EXCELLENT DOCTOR. PLEASE COME TO MY COURT AND BECOME THE ROYAL PHYSICIAN.

I AM HONOURED!

AZIZUDDIN ROSE FAST AND SOON BECAME RANJIT SINGH'S CONFIDENTIAL ADVISER.

TELL ME, AZIZUDDIN, WHAT DO YOU THINK OF THESE RELIGIOUS DIFFERENCES IN OUR LAND?

SIRE, I AM LIKE A MAN FLOATING IN THE MIDST OF A MIGHTY RIVER. I TURN MY EYES TOWARDS THE LAND, BUT CAN DISTINGUISH NO DIFFERENCE IN EITHER BANK.

TRULY YOU ARE A WISE AND TOLERANT MAN. WE SHALL HENCEFORTH CALL YOU FAKIR AZIZUDDIN!

FAKIR AZIZUDDIN EVENTUALLY BECAME RANJIT SINGH'S FOREIGN MINISTER.

ANOTHER OF RANJIT SINGH'S MINISTERS WAS DINA NATH, A KASHMIRI HINDU, WHO LOOKED AFTER THE FINANCES OF THE STATE.

I NEED MORE MONEY FOR THE ARMY.

DON'T WORRY, SIRE. THE MERCHANTS AND BUSINESSMEN WILL CONTRIBUTE TO THE TREASURY IN RETURN FOR THE PEACE AND SECURITY YOUR REIGN HAS BROUGHT THEM.

RANJIT SINGH'S MOST FAMOUS GENERAL WAS HARI SINGH NALWA, A SIKH, WHO REPEATEDLY DEFEATED THE AFGHANS.

HE WAS ALWAYS IN THE THICK OF BATTLE...

...AN INSPIRATION TO HIS SOLDIERS...

...AND AN OBJECT OF FEAR TO HIS ENEMIES.

IT'S HARI SINGH NALWA.

RUN! WE DON'T STAND A CHANCE.

21

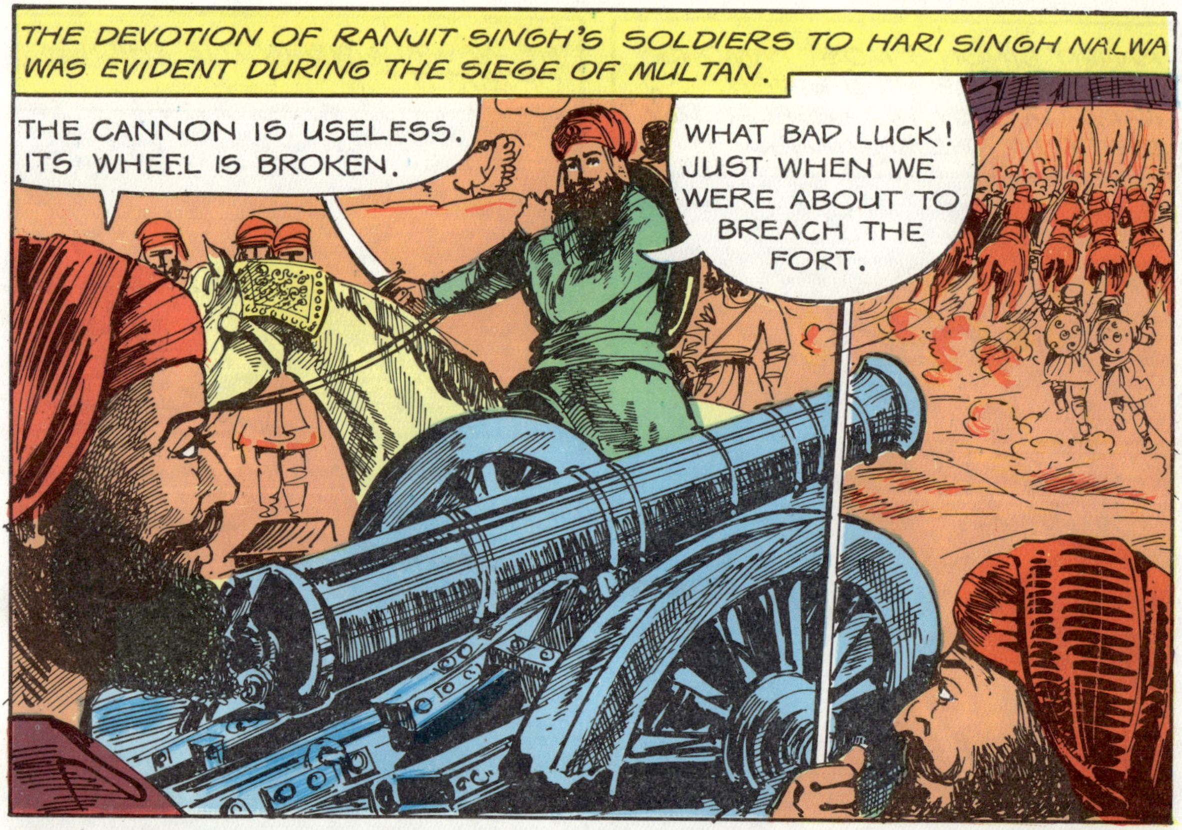

THE DEVOTION OF RANJIT SINGH'S SOLDIERS TO HARI SINGH NALWA WAS EVIDENT DURING THE SIEGE OF MULTAN.

THE CANNON IS USELESS. ITS WHEEL IS BROKEN.

WHAT BAD LUCK! JUST WHEN WE WERE ABOUT TO BREACH THE FORT.

THERE IS NO TIME TO REPAIR IT. WE WILL HAVE TO WITHDRAW!

WAIT! I WILL SUPPORT THE CANNON ON MY BACK.

SO WILL I! SO WILL I!

23

A BREACH WAS MADE. INSPIRED BY THE SACRIFICES, THE SIKH ARMY STORMED INTO THE CITADEL.

FORWARD!

VICTORY IS OURS!

AFTER MULTAN, PESHAWAR AND KASHMIR FELL TO THE SIKH ARMY.

HE FOUGHT BRAVELY BUT WAS FINALLY OVERCOME.

MY END IS NEAR. BUT DO NOT DISCLOSE THIS. KEEP FIGHTING!

THOUGH LEADERLESS, THE SIKHS KEPT FIGHTING UNTIL—

THE MAHARAJA IS HERE.

FOR RANJIT, ANOTHER VICTORY WAS TINGED WITH SADNESS. NALWA FELL IN THE BATTLE.

I HAVE LOST MY MOST LOYAL AND FAITHFUL WARRIOR!

ANOTHER OF RANJIT SINGH'S GENERALS, ZORAWAR SINGH, CONQUERED LADAKH AND MARCHED INTO THE HEART OF TIBET.

RANJIT SINGH'S FAME SPREAD ALL OVER THE WORLD. IN FRANCE THE KING HEARD ABOUT HIM FROM A FRENCH TRAVELLER.

YOUR EXCELLENCY, A NEW CONQUEROR AND STATESMAN HAS ARISEN IN HINDUSTAN; RANJIT SINGH, THE LION OF THE PUNJAB.

GOOD! PERHAPS HE WILL DEFEAT THE BRITISH AND BECOME OUR ALLY.

THE BRITISH WERE ALARMED BY RANJIT SINGH'S SUCCESS.

THIS MAN RANJIT SINGH IS BECOMING TOO POWERFUL. WHAT SHALL WE DO!

A STRONG ARTILLERY CORPS, WITH CANNONS AND GUNNERS WAS ALSO FORMED.

THE CAVALRY, THE MAIN STRIKING FORCE, WAS STRENGTHENED.

SOLDIERS OF FORTUNE, FROM OUTSIDE THE PUNJAB FLOCKED TO RANJIT SINGH'S ARMY_ NOTABLY THE GURKHAS.

ONE OF THE CROWNING ACHIEVEMENTS OF RANJIT SINGH'S REIGN WAS HIS ACQUISITION OF THE FAMED KOH-I-NOOR DIAMOND.

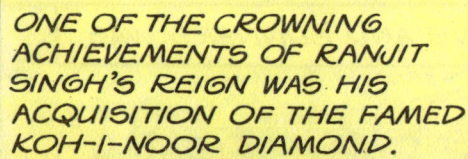

IT WAS SUPPOSED TO HAVE BEEN WORN BY THE PANDAVA KINGS.

AND IN MUGHAL TIMES IT ADORNED THE PEACOCK THRONE.

BUT WITH RANJIT SINGH'S CONQUEST OF KASHMIR, SHAH SHUJAH WAS FORCED TO HAND IT OVER TO THE SIKH KING.

SIRE, IT IS YOURS. THE BIGGEST DIAMOND IN THE WORLD.

NADIR SHAH TOOK IT AWAY WHEN HE SACKED DELHI.

RANJIT SINGH'S REIGN WAS NOW DRAWING TO AN END. IN 1837 HIS GRANDSON, NAU NIHAL SINGH WAS MARRIED AMIDST GREAT SPLENDOUR.

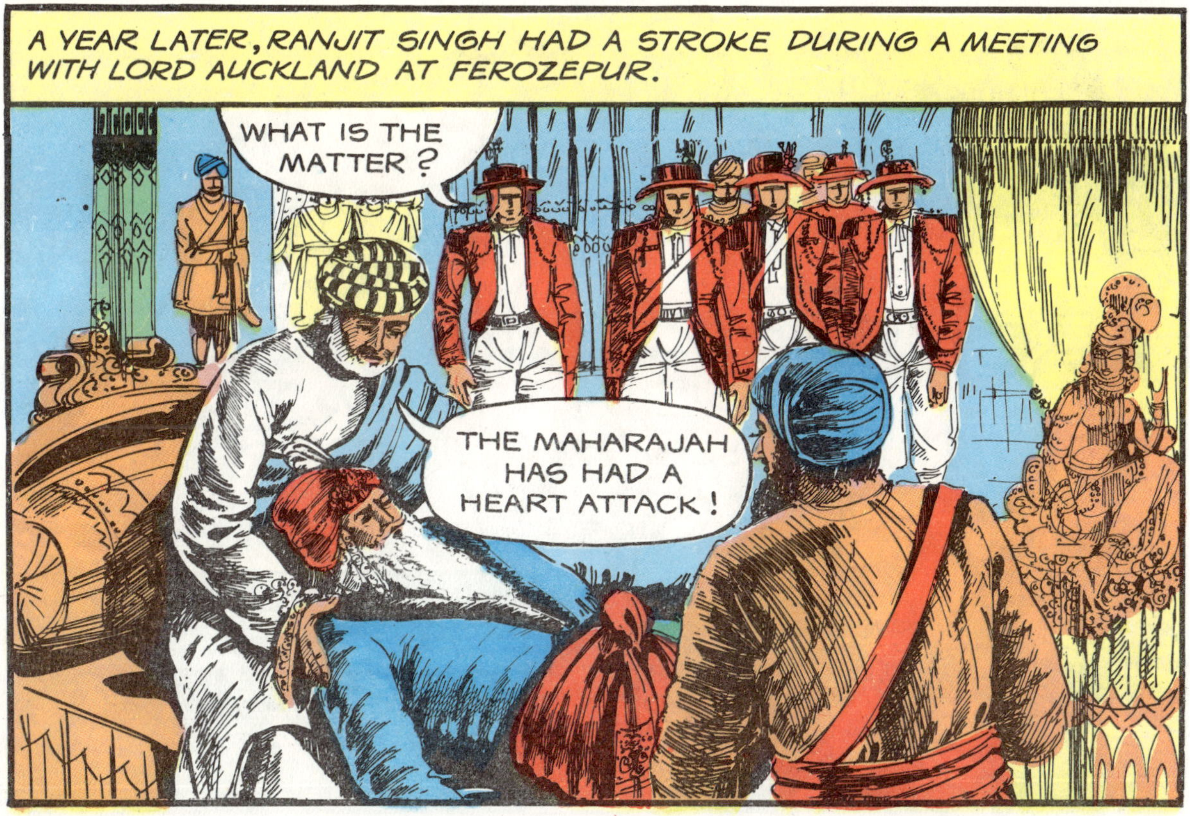

A YEAR LATER, RANJIT SINGH HAD A STROKE DURING A MEETING WITH LORD AUCKLAND AT FEROZEPUR.

WHAT IS THE MATTER?

THE MAHARAJAH HAS HAD A HEART ATTACK!

ON JUNE 27, 1839, RANJIT SINGH BREATHED HIS LAST.

A SANDALWOOD PYRE WAS LIT AND HIS RANIS COMMITTED 'SATI' BY THROWING THEMSELVES INTO THE FIRE.